Hardback ISBN: 979-8-9898164-0-8
eBook ISBN: 979-8-9898164-1-5

Edited by Mary March

Published by Degu Press
Aurora, CO
www.degupress.org

Springhare
Makes Some Friends

Kelsey Kopecky

Hi there! I'm a **Springhare**!

SPRINGHARE
(pronounced like spring-hair)

There aren't many other rodents like me.

I have big ears, giant feet,
and a very very long tail!

I love to go exploring–

GUNDI
(pronounced like GOON-dee)

These are my friends!

We all have big back feet, and our ears sort of match, but we're still different. Our tails are unique and I'm much bigger than both of you.

I wonder if there's anyone else out there that's also like a Springhare...

Spring-<u>hare</u>?
We know a hare!

This is our friend, the **Hare**!

Hare, meet Springhare!

They were wondering if you were like them?

HARE
(pronounced like hair)

We are a bit similar, but I like to run on only my back legs instead of on all four.

And while we may have a similar name, you are a rodent and I'm not.

Oh I don't know if I'll ever
find someone else quite like me...

Don't worry!

I know someone we can ask.

They know a lot of other rodents!

Sorry to wake you!
I was just wondering if you
knew about other rodents like me?

It's okay!
I'm happy to help of course,
and I know who we should ask.

You'll find my friend down
in that pool of water.
They'll definitely be able to help you.
They're the wisest animal I know!

CAPYBARA
(pronounced like ka-pee-BEAR-uh)

I'm looking for other rodents that are the same as me. But everyone that I've found is a little bit different.

You are quite unique, Springhare.

And so is everyone else.

I'm not sure you'll ever find someone the same as you, but that's okay because you seem to have found plenty of friends along the way.

Learn more about real springhares and the other animals in this book at your local library or online at www.degupress.org/springhare

Printed in the USA
CPSIA information can be obtained
at www.ICGtesting.com
JSRC080828110224
56721JS00018B/23

979898981640 8